BEGINNER READER

Dante
the
Flying
Dragon

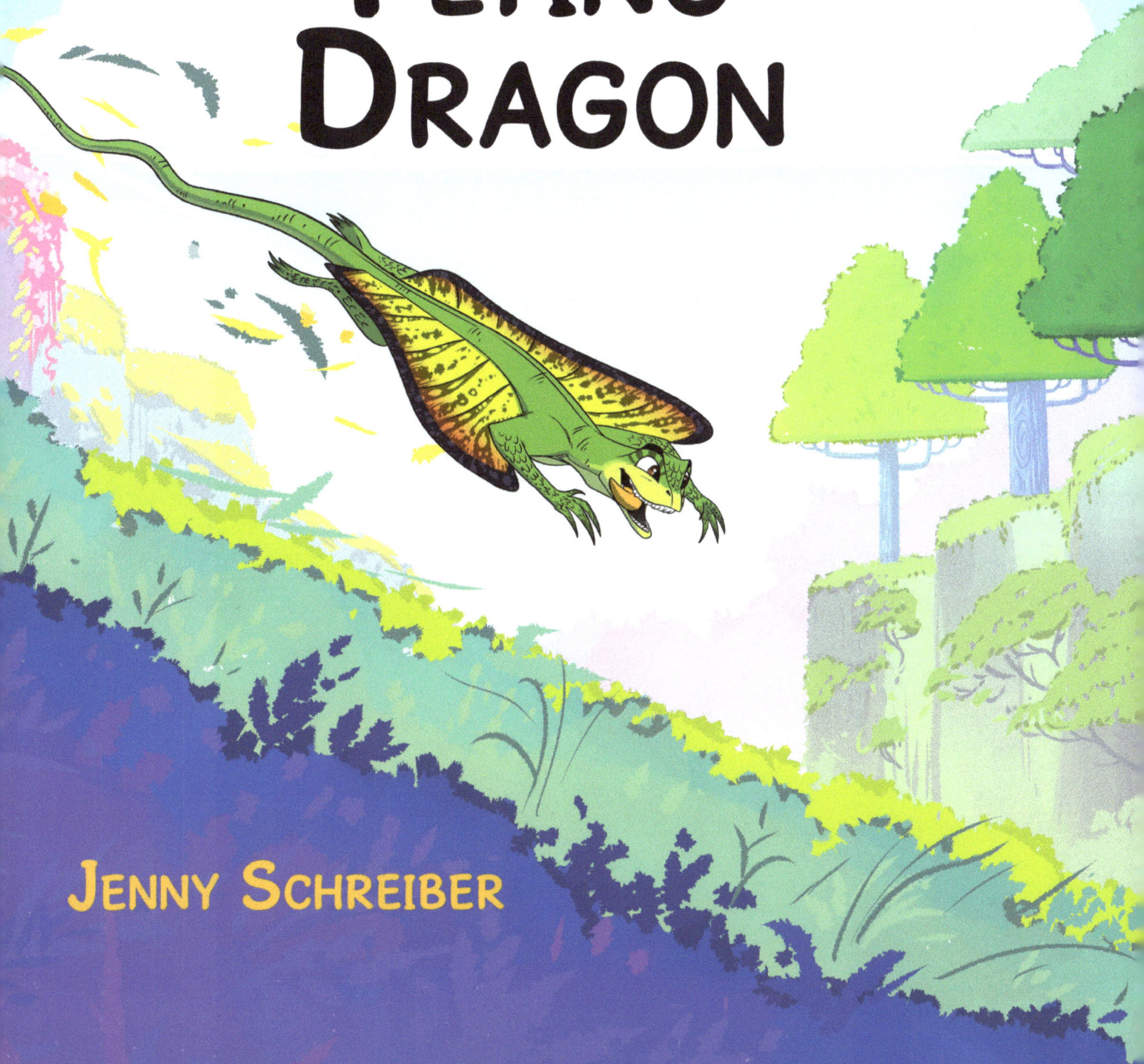

Jenny Schreiber

Dante the Flying Dragon

©2024 Jenny Schreiber

In Association with:
Elite Online Publishing
63 East 11400 South
Suite #230
Sandy, UT 84070
EliteOnlinePublishing.com

ISBN: 978-1-961801-35-6 (Paperback)
ISBN: 978-1-961801-36-3 (Hardback)
ISBN: 978-1-961801-37-0 (eBook)

Quantity purchases: Schools, companies, professional groups, clubs, and other organizations may qualify for special terms when ordering bulk quantities of this title. For information, email info@eliteonlinepublishing.com.

This book is printed in the United States of America.

DANTE

THE

FLYING

DRAGON

JENNY SCHREIBER

MEET DANTE THE FLYING DRAGON

DANTE IS A DRACO VOLANS LIZARD, WITH LONG
WINGS THAT STRETCH FROM HIS ARMS TO HIS LEGS.

DRACO LIZARDS ARE ALSO CALLED "FLYING DRAGONS" BECAUSE THEY LOOK LIKE MYTHICAL CREATURES IN CHINESE LEGENDS.

DANTE IS VERY LIGHT, HE ONLY WEIGHS ABOUT **20** GRAMS OR HALF A POUND.

DANTE USES HIS WINGS TO GLIDE FROM TREE TO TREE, LIKE A PAPER AIRPLANE.

DANTE HAS A
BRIGHT GREEN COLOR THAT HELPS
HIM BLEND INTO THE LEAVES OF TREES.

When Dante spreads his wings, he has a wingspan of up to **30** cm or about **12** inches.

HE HAS A LONG TAIL THAT ACTS
AS A RUDDER, HELPING HIM
STEER WHILE GLIDING.

DANTE IS A VERY FAST GLIDER AND
CAN REACH SPEEDS OF UP TO 60 KM/H
OR ABOUT 37 MP/H.

DANTE HAS SHARP CLAWS THAT HELP HIM TO GRIP TREE BRANCHES.

Dante can climb fast up trees using his sharp claws and long tail.

DANTE IS AN OMNIVORE AND EATS
INSECTS, FRUITS, AND FLOWERS.

DANTE HAS EXCELLENT
EYESIGHT AND CAN SPOT PREY
FROM HIGH UP IN THE TREES.

DANTE LIVES IN SOUTHEAST ASIA,
FROM THAILAND TO INDONESIA.

He prefers to live in tropical rainforests with lots of trees.

DANTE IS TERRITORIAL AND WILL DEFEND HIS SPACE FROM OTHER LIZARDS.

DANTE LIVES UP TO **8** YEARS IN THE WILD.

DANTE IS NOT ENDANGERED BUT
THE FORESTS IN SOUTHEAST ASIA
ARE BEING DESTROYED WHICH MEANS
THERE ARE FEWER OF THEM.

Even though Dante is small, he has an adventurous spirit and looks like he is part lizard, part butterfly.

THE END

POSES

← INK & COLORS

SKETCHES

DANTE
THE DRACO VOLANS LIZARD

Find More books by Jenny Schreiber

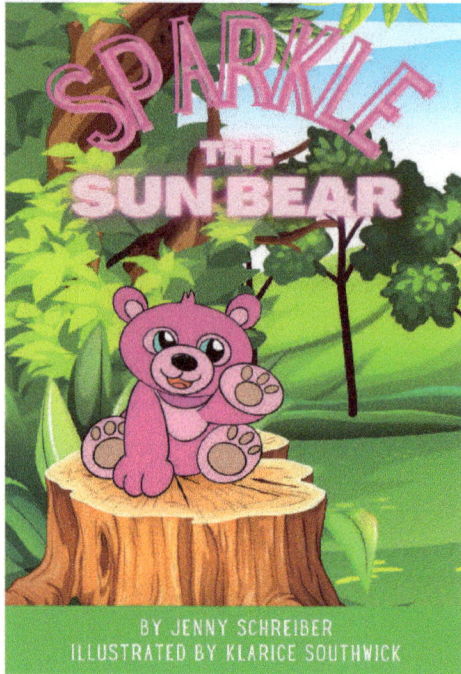

Sparkle the Sun Bear

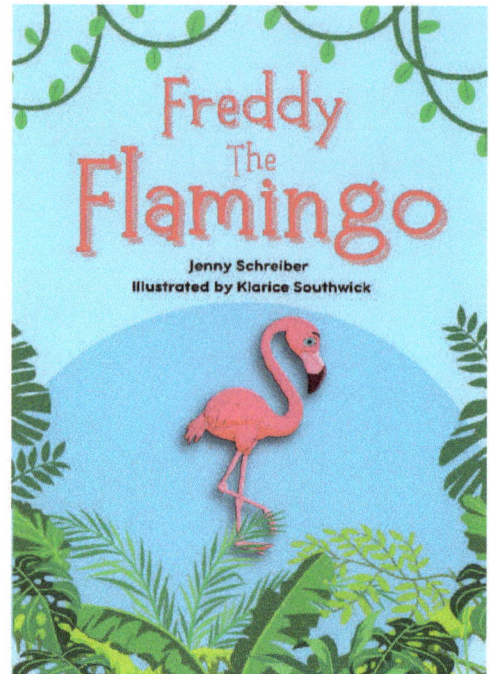

Freddy the Flamingo

Piper the
Polar Bear

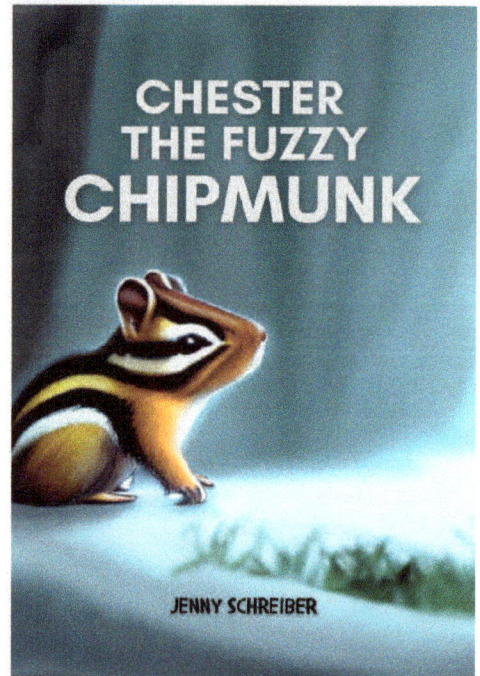

Chester the
Fuzzy Chipmunk

Animal Facts Children's Book Series

Paige the
Panda Bear

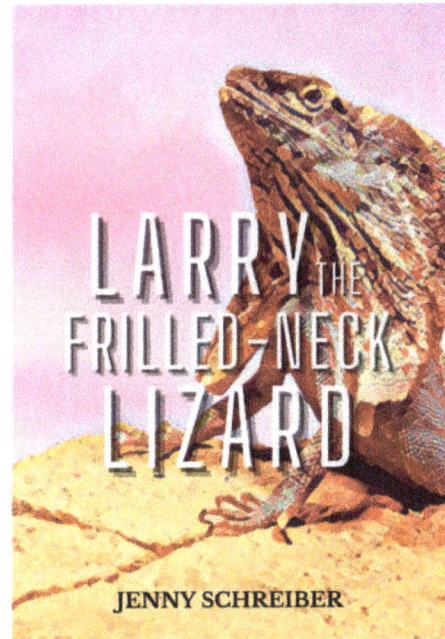

Larry the
Frilled-Neck Lizard

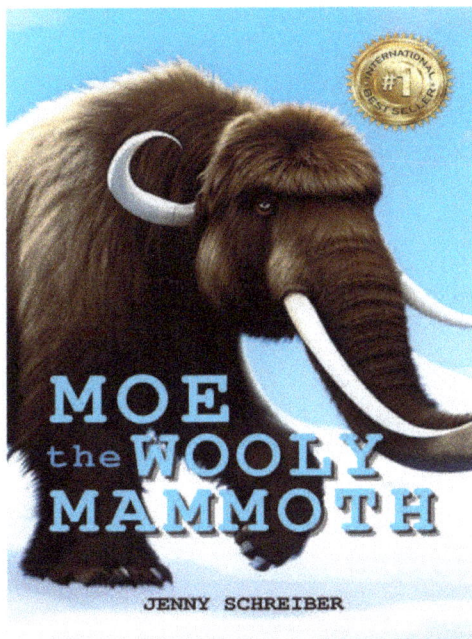

Moe the
Wooly Mammoth

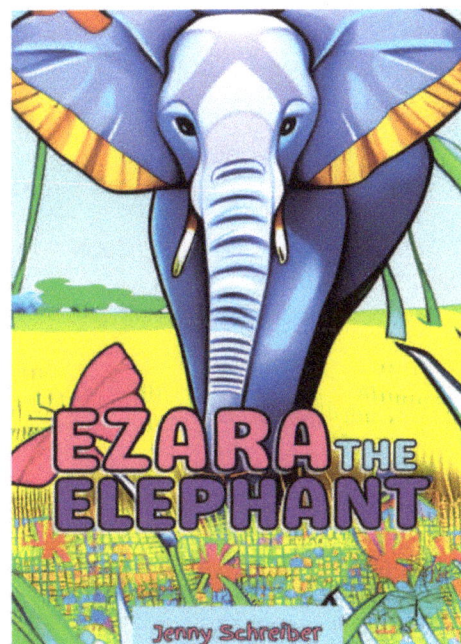

Ezara the
Elephant

Animal Facts Children's Book Series

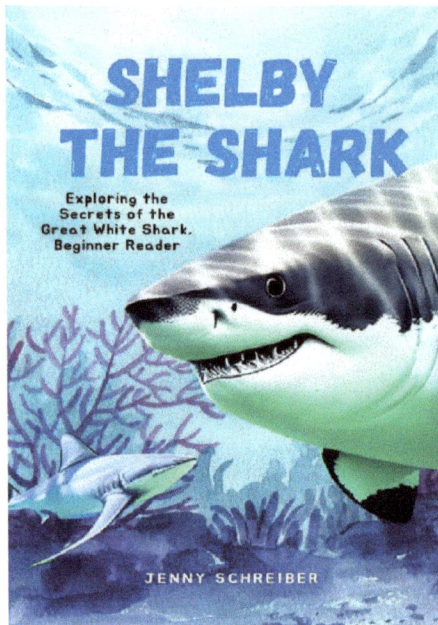

Shelby the Shark

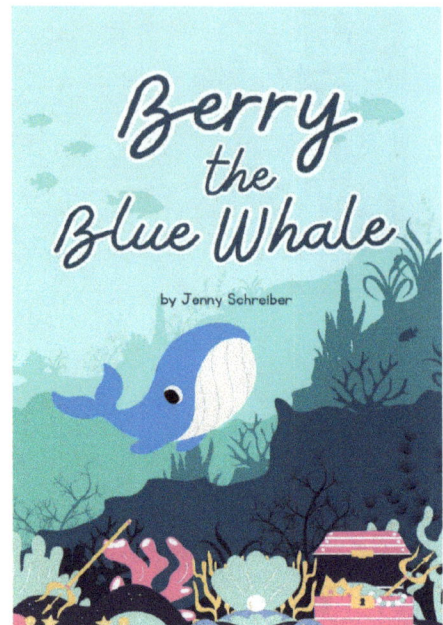

Berry the
Blue Whale

Loxi the Lop
Eared Bunny

www.ingramcontent.com/pod-product-compliance
Lightning Source LLC
Chambersburg PA
CBHW042344030426
42335CB00030B/3454